HERMELIN

the Detective Mouse

Mini Grey

Alfred A. Knopf ⬥ New York

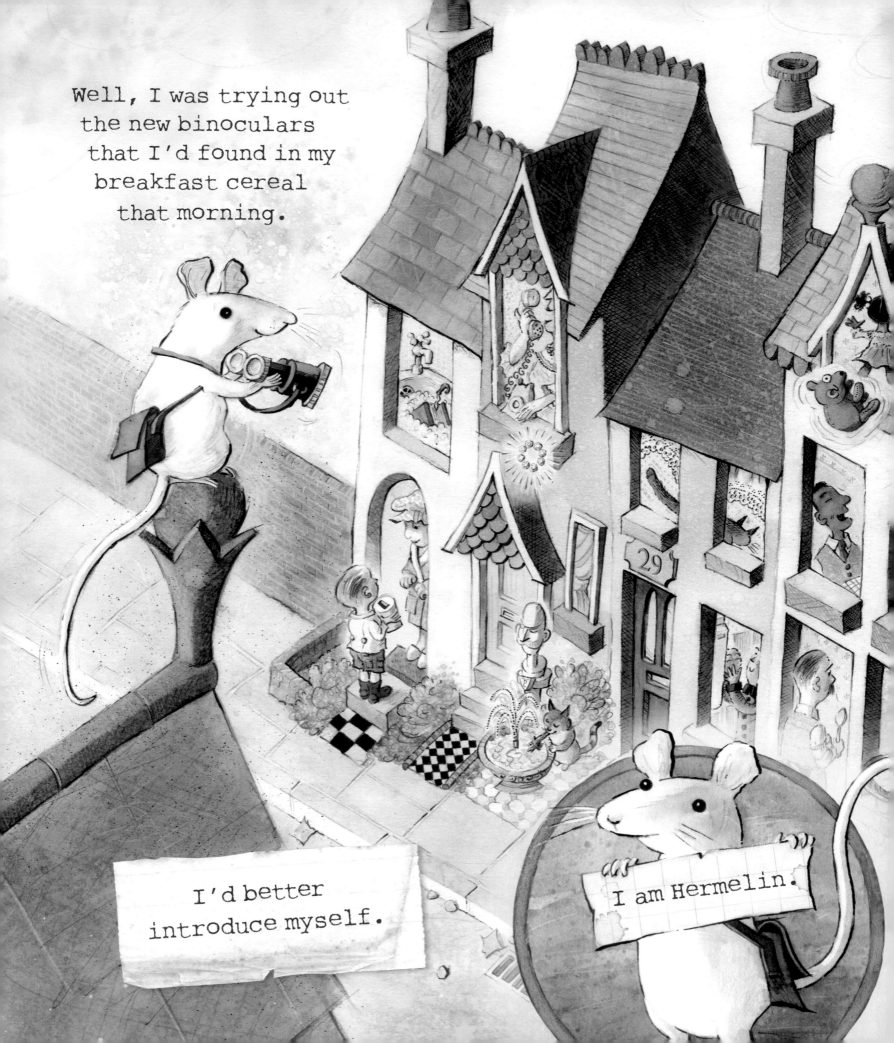

Well, I was trying out the new binoculars that I'd found in my breakfast cereal that morning.

I'd better introduce myself.

I am Hermelin.

The first thing I can
remember is waking up
in my cheese box (which smelled
delicious) and finding
I could read the name on it.

It said:

HERMELIN

So I knew

that was what

I was called.

READY SALTED

Then I found this attic.
It is at the top of
Number 33 Offley Street.

It is full of
books and boxes
and boots,
and also
a typewriter.

Well, it was just after lunchtime on Offley Street,
and I was passing the OFFLEY STREET NOTICE BOARD,
and I had a good look at it.

OFFLEY STREET

LOST BAG It belongs to Mrs. Mattison. Black leather containing life savings. Tel: 0207 946 0265

GONE! Have you seen my Teddy BoBo? He is maybe Lost. Tell Imogen Splotts.

Desperately Seeking **PARSLEY**

Greenish fur. Distinguished meow. Partial to fish. Greatly missed. Reports to Captain Potts, 31 Offley St.

Missing! My reading glasses have disappeared. If found, notify Dr. Parker at No. 25

DISAPPEARED!

MY BELOVED GOLDFISH **LUCKY** IS GONE FROM HIS BOWL Any sightings, contact Bernardo Bosher at

BOSHER'S SAUSAGE SHOP 37 OFFLEY STREET

TELECOM

NOTICES

MAN
WiTH
VAN
call Andy
0770090843

VANISHED!
My priceless Diamond Bracelet
is LOST (perhaps stolen)

GENEROUS REWARD
No Questions Asked
Contact Lady Chumley-Plumley

Have you seen
my notebook?
I would really like it back –
contains vital information.
Emily
at No. 33
P.S. To whoever is
eating my cornflakes –
Help yourself!

I thought to myself:

Great
heavens!

Just LOOK
at all these
lost things!

THESE

POOR PEOPLE

OF

OFFLEY STREET

NEED

SOME

HELP!

And I knew
I was exactly the one
for the job.

So I got to work.

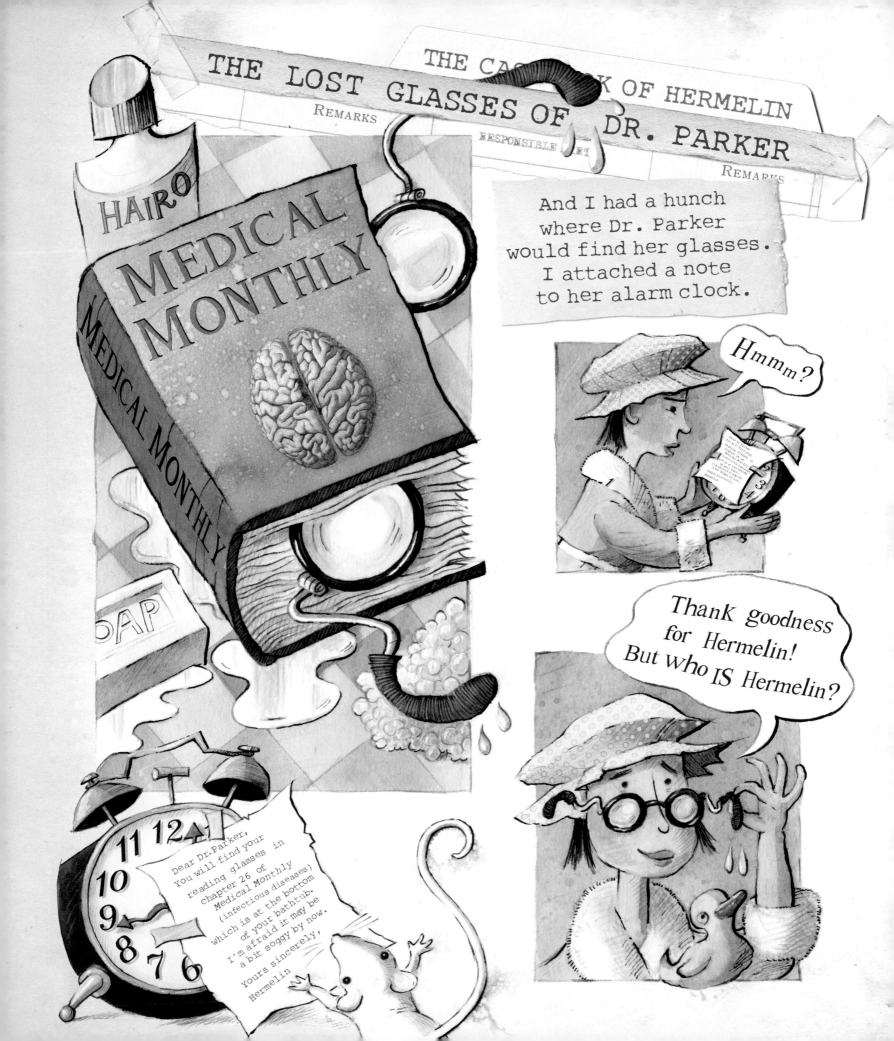

I dropped a note onto
Imogen Splotts's pillow...

Dear Young Imogen Splotts,

Bobo your Bear has crash-landed
in the lemon meringue pie
that Captain Potts has left out
to cool. He may well be sticky,
but he will smell nice.
          Yours,
            Hermelin

Dear Bernardo,
LUCKY, your beloved goldfish,
    is currently in
Lady Chumley-Plumley's
        fountain,
   being cruelly taunted
   by Parsley the cat.
I'd hurry if I were you!
            Yours,
              Hermelin

...and taped another to
Bernardo Bosher's
empty goldfish bowl...

GARBAGE GOBBLER

There's no time to type,
but maybe I can
use the notebook.

Dear McMumbo,
Please Hurry
BABY McMUMBO
is in trash AND
IN PeriL!
Hermelin

I struggle with the stubby
pencil; my paws are not good
at this sort of thing.

FOLD
FOLD

When the message is written,
I fold it as quick as I can . . .

. . . into an airplane shape
that will fly well,

and with the last of my strength,
I hurl the plane toward
Mr. McMumbo's open window . . .

Mr. McMumbo just manages to reach the Munch-u-lator Automatic Garbage Gobbler in time.

On Friday I saw there was a report in Emily's *Offley Times*.

INVITATION

Dear Hermelin,

We don't know who you are, but you have helped everybody – and you have saved the life of Baby McMumbo.

Please come to a

THANK-YOU PARTY IN YOUR HONOR

at Bosher's sausage Shop
at 4pm this afternoon.

Everybody wants to meet you!

Yours gratefully,
The People of
Offley Street

I spent some time in my attic smartening up my fur.

Quite a crowd
had gathered in
Bosher's sausage shop.

I felt very nervous
but took a deep breath
and stepped forward to say
Hello.

A Mouse. But what's so bad about being a mouse?

572

mourn
mourn (mörn) v.i. & t. Feel sorrow or regret (for or over dead person, lost thing, loss, misfortune, etc.)

mousaka or **moussaka** /mooh'sahka/ noun a Greek dish consisting of layers of minced lamb or other meat, aubergine, tomato, and cheese with a cheese or savoury custard topping. [Modern Greek mousakas from Turkish musakka]

mouse. (pl. **mice**)
1a small rodent infesting houses etc.; with a pointed snout, and a long slender almost hairless tail: family Muridae. The House Mouse (Mus Musculus) has been carried around the world by Man. This **pest** causes **untold** damage annually to foods and materials.

heart   intestines

lungs

House mouse: mus musculus Famil
Mice may carry bacteria, viruses a
L. mūs, Gr. mŷs, Skr. mūs-.
'**steal, rob**'.

573   **mouse**

play **cat and mouse with**, torment with suspense; **mouse~'trap**, for catching mice; **mouse** ~trap cheese, of poor quality ; timid shy person ; **mou'sŷ**
2. (or ~z) v.i. (Of cat, owl, etc.) hunt mice.
3. (pl. also **mouses**) in computing, a small box, with a movable ball under it, that is connected to a computer and that, when moved across a desk or mat, causes a cursor to move across a VDU screen, so enabling the operator to point to and execute commands.
Albinos - white mice - are valuable research animals.

See also:
PESTS AND DISEASES

moustache
mous'tache, *mus-, (mus'tahh) n. Hair on either side (usu. in pl.) or both sides of (usu. man's) upper lip.

MOUSTACHE. The hair on a man's upper lip when allowed to grow.

I ran for my life, leaving a trail of crumbs and cream behind me.

Back in my attic I consulted the encyclopedia. Unclean, Unhygienic, Unwanted. The devastating truth was . . .

fig. *A*

Silverfish

Cockroach

fig. *B*

fig. *C*

Tick

I was a PEST.

HOUSEHOLD

I felt suddenly very alone.
It was time to leave
Offley Street.

I packed up
some things
to take with me
in the morning . . .

ERMELIN

and then
sadly went to
sleep in my cheese box.

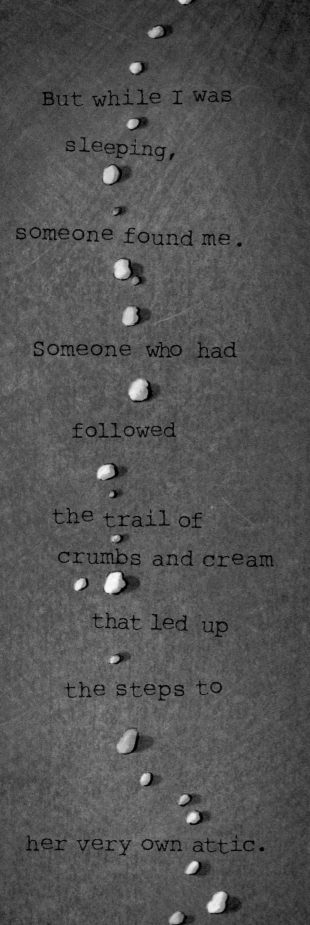

But while I was

sleeping,

someone found me.

Someone who had

followed

the trail of

crumbs and cream

that led up

the steps to

her very own attic.

And that someone

had a good look around,

and then took out
a mouse-sized note
and tucked it
into my cheese box.

Detective mouse needed
with good typing skills.
Could you be the one I'm looking for?
If so, come down to breakfast
with me – Emily
I'm waiting!

And now I have breakfast every day in the kitchen downstairs at Number 33 with Emily (who says she is a bit of a detective, too).

We read the cereal boxes
and the newspaper, and

we hunt carefully for clues,

because we have a plan
to start a
DETECTIVE AGENCY...

Hermelin & Emily

PRIVATE
INVESTIGATORS

You name it – we can solve it!

. . . as Emily suspects there are still a few mysteries to be solved around Offley Street.